Dear Reader,

I, Nate the Great, am a detective.
Sometimes I work on cases with
my cousin Olivia Sharp.
She's an Agent for Secrets.
What is an Agent for Secrets?
Olivia will tell you all about it.
She works hard on her cases.
She's here. She's there.
She's everywhere.
She whizzes around the streets
of San Francisco.
Follow her!
I, Nate the Great,
say that you will have
a very good time.

Yours truly,

 Nate the Great

Olivia Sharp

THE SLY SPY

by Marjorie Weinman Sharmat
and Mitchell Sharmat
illustrated by Denise Brunkus

A YEARLING BOOK

Published by
Yearling
an imprint of
Random House Children's Books
a division of Random House, Inc.
New York

Visit us on the Web! www.randomhouse.com/kids

Educators and librarians, for a variety of teaching tools, visit us at
www.randomhouse.com/teachers

ISBN: 0-440-42062-8 (pbk.)   ISBN: 0-385-90292-1 (lib. bdg.)

Reprinted by arrangement with Delacorte Press

Printed in the United States of America

Second Yearling Edition June 2005

10 9 8 7 6 5 4 3

OPM

For Craig
—M.W.S. and M.S.

For Josephine Olivia
—D.B.

This Is Me

My name is Olivia
Sharp.

I'm a special
kind of detective.

I'm an agent for secrets.

If you have a secret problem, call me.

I work out of my penthouse on top of Pacific Heights in San Francisco.

Wanted: New Clients

Let me tell you about my last case. It began on a Saturday.

The week had been slow. The red phone in my office hadn't rung in days. My desk was clean. I was trying to figure out what I could do to drum up business.

I decided to hit the streets and see who I could find who needed help.

I grabbed my boa and rang for my chauffeur, Willie, to bring the limo around.

Then I went to the elevator and pressed the button.

chapter three
Mystery Boy

When the elevator came I stepped inside.
There was a boy standing in the corner.
The elevator started down. The boy slid
his eyes sideways to look me over.

5

I had never seen him before. I could
hardly see him now. A big hat was pulled
down over his face. He was wearing a
raincoat, even though it wasn't raining.
He looked like *he* needed help. With his
clothes, if nothing else.

"My name is Olivia Sharp," I said.

"Hello, Liver."

We were *not* off to a good start!

"I'm an agent for secrets," I said. "You may have heard of me. I'm almost famous. Here's my card."

"That's stupid," he said. He pushed his hat up. He had green eyes that glittered like a Halloween cat's.

"*Stupid* is a stupid word," I said. I fluffed my boa and turned my back on him.

When the elevator reached the ground

floor, he just stood there. Maybe he lived in the elevator. I didn't want to. I got out.

Willie was waiting at the curb with the limo.

"Where to, Boss?" he asked as we rolled out of the courtyard, through the big iron gates, and onto Steiner Street.

"Cruise the streets. We're looking for clients, Willie."

Willie drove us around and around. And up and down.

This was *soooo* ho-hum.

I started to think about my cousin, Nate the Great. He's a detective, too.

But he doesn't have to look for clients.

He gets his cases whether he wants them or not.

chapter four

The Feathered Present

Twenty minutes later I spotted some kids going into the grocery store on Union Street. "Pull over," I said.

I went into the grocery store while Willie

parked the limo. I headed for the vegetable department. You can get a good view of the store from there.

I was turning over some mushrooms when someone tapped me on the shoulder.

I knew it was Sheena, even before I
looked. All I had to do was sniff. Sheena
uses a shampoo that smells like macaroons.

"Am I glad you're here!" she said. "I
need your help."

I didn't want to let on that I was desperate for a new case. And besides, it doesn't look classy to pick up clients while you're feeling vegetables.

"What kind of help?" I asked coolly.

Sheena leaned closer to me. "It's about Desiree's birthday. Duncan, Mortimer, and I told Desiree we wanted to chip in for one nice present for her party tomorrow. We asked her for a hint about what she'd like. She said, 'I love feathers.' So we bought Desiree a canary."

"A *canary*?"

"Yes. A canary has lots of feathers."

"Right. So what's the secret problem?"

"The canary is. We want the canary to be a secret until Desiree's party. Mortimer

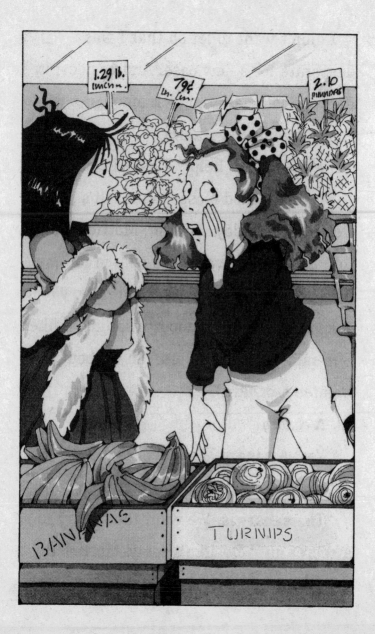

took it home. But Desiree went to his house and started looking around. That's not fair! A secret is supposed to be a secret."

"I guess Desiree just can't wait to see what you got her. But if she finds out she'll spoil her own surprise. She didn't see the canary, did she?"

Sheena smiled. "No, it was lucky that Duncan had come by to take it out for a walk."

"Duncan took a canary for a *walk*?" I couldn't believe what I was hearing. I lifted my boa out of a bin of broccoli.

"Yes. Duncan says canaries need fresh air. So he took it out, cage and all."

"Go on."

"Well, since Desiree had been snooping

around Mortimer's house, Duncan said he'd keep the canary at *his* house."

"That didn't solve your problem?" I asked.

"No. Desiree went to Duncan's house! Good thing I was there. I grabbed the canary cage and sneaked down the back stairs before Desiree could see the canary and me. And here we are!"

"*We?*"

Sheena pointed to the floor. Behind her was a canary cage! Sheena kept pointing. "I can't take him home because I know Desiree will come over. She'll keep going to Mortimer's and Duncan's and my house until she catches one of us with the canary."

"Let me get this straight," I said. "Your problem is that you have no place to keep the canary until Desiree's birthday party?"

"That's it," Sheena said. "This can be your new case."

This was a *case*? No way.

It was a thousand yawns!

chapter five
The Missing Ad

But I wanted to help Sheena and Mortimer and Duncan. But how? Then I had an idea.

"I'm good with birds," I said. "I already have my pet owl, Hoot. And I have lots of room. I'll keep the canary until Desiree's party tomorrow. And I'll keep it a secret."

Sheena handed me the birdcage.

"His name is Feathers. He's named for Desiree's hint."

"Good to know," I said.

Sheena walked away.

I said, "I usually don't do business over vegetables. I have an office, I have a desk, I have files, I have a red telephone. I have ads all over town with my telephone number on them."

I pointed to the bulletin board near the front of the store. "I even have an ad in this store."

"Not anymore," Sheena said. "I checked for it, but it's gone."

"Gone? How can it be gone?"

Sheena shrugged and walked away.

chapter six

I Spy, You Spy

I rushed to the bulletin board. I looked at
the spot where I had put up my ad. I saw
an ad. But it wasn't mine! It said:

E.J.'s Spy Service.
I will spy for you.
CALL ME DAY OR NIGHT.
555-4133

I lifted a corner of the ad and looked under it.

My ad was still there! Hidden. This E. J. person had covered it up.

I pulled down E.J.'s ad and put it in my pocketbook. *I* was going to call 555-4133! There was plenty of room for both of our ads, so why had E.J. covered *mine*?

I left the store with the canary and the spy ad.

"Nice bird, Boss," Willie said.

Willie drove us home.

The elevator was empty this time.
Maybe Mr. Stupid had a hobby of riding in
elevators and he had gone on to another
building. I could only hope.

chapter seven

The Overnight Guest

I introduced Feathers to my housekeeper, Mrs. Fridgeflake.

"We have an overnight guest," I said.

Then I went to Hoot's room and said,
"I've got a friend for you, Hoot."

Hoot looked at Feathers. It was not a
friendly look. It was a hungry look.

I decided to give Feathers his own room.

I put him in the yellow room, which matched his feathers. It's my parents' room, but I knew they wouldn't mind since they were in Stockholm, Sweden, that week. I wished they would come home soon.

"This room belongs to Wilfred and Maude. They're my parents," I said to Feathers. "So behave yourself."

I went to my office
to call 555-4133.

But my red telephone
rang first.

Maybe a real client at last!

"**O**livia Sharp,
Agent for Secrets," I answered.

"Your world is coming to an end," a voice
said.

It was Duncan.

"*My* world is coming to an end?" I asked.

"Yes. I just saw four of your ads covered over with some kind of spy ad. Now *you're* the one who has a problem. Can I help?"

"*Four* of my ads?"

This was spreading! Pretty soon all my ads would be hidden. Maybe they were already.

No wonder business was bad!

"I'll look into it," I said. "Thanks."

chapter nine
Thinking Time

I put down the receiver. Then I picked it up
and dialed 555-4133.

After the fifth ring I heard a boy's
voice announce, "This is E.J.'s Spy Service.

I will be glad to spy for you, but I am
not here right now. Leave your
number."

An answering machine! I refuse to talk
to machines. I slammed down the receiver.

I went to my furry white chair, sat down,
and looked out the window. There was no

fog over San Francisco Bay, and I could see the boats moving back and forth past Alcatraz Island.

I thought about the boy's voice on the answering machine. The sound of the *s* in *Spy* and *Service*. I had heard that *s* before. But where?

I sank deeper into my chair. But not for long. I heard *chirp, chirp, chirp*.

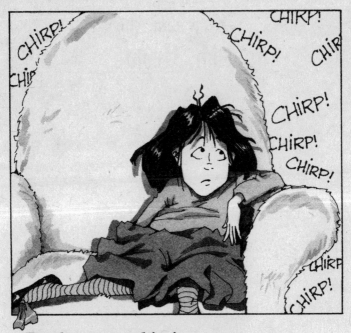

Feathers was chirping away.

Chirp, chirp, chirp. Nonstop. Noisy bird!

That's what I like about an owl. It only gives a hoot now and then.

Maybe Feathers was hungry. What do you feed a canary?

chapter ten
Mr. Stupid

I grabbed my boa and the canary cage.
I rang for Willie to bring the limo
around.

"To the Feathered Friends Pet Shop,"

I said as I settled into the backseat with
Feathers.

It only took five minutes to get there.
Feathers chirped all the way.

The store was full of feathery pets.

One of them looked like my boa.

I made my way past a goose, a duck, a chicken, a parrot, and a canary.

I held up my canary cage.

"I'll have one day's supply of whatever

this creature eats," I said to a lady behind the counter.

I bought the pet food and fed Feathers on the spot.

Then we went home.

Willie parked the limo while I got into the elevator with Feathers.

Mr. Stupid was there!

He pulled his collar up and his hat down.

"Is that your canary?" he asked as the elevator started up.

"This isn't a canary," I said. "This is actually an elephant, pretending to be a canary."

"That's stupid," he said.

"Just a minute," I said. "That's two

stupids too many. Who do you think you are, anyway?"

The elevator jerked to a stop at the fourth floor.

"So long, Liver," he said, and he got off.

He walked to the door of the apartment just opposite the elevator. My best friend, Taffy Plimpton, had lived in that apartment before she moved away to Carmel.
Mr. Stupid must have moved in!

"Wait!" I called.

But the elevator door closed.

chapter eleven

Agent vs. Spy

*S*uddenly I knew who he *really* was!
When he said *stupid,* the *s* had leapt up
and nudged my brain. *S* as in *Spy*
Service. This boy was E.J., the person

who had covered my ads and spoiled
my business!

When the elevator
reached my floor, I
went straight to my
office and dialed
555-4133.

This time E.J. answered. "E.J., the spy who's sly, at your service."

"This is Olivia Sharp, Agent for Secrets, and I know yours. You live on the fourth floor of my building."

"So what?" he said.

"So this," I said. "You've been going around town covering up my ads. Why?"

"You're an
agent for
secrets. I'm a spy.
You figure it out."

I figured it out and I
didn't like it.

"Can't talk," he said. "I'm busy with a
big case."

This kid was unreal. I yawned and said,
"Oh, really? You've got an actual case?"

"Right. So long, Liver."

He hung up.

I don't believe in war, but E.J. was
beginning to give the idea a good name.
He hadn't heard the last of me.

chapter twelve

The Decoy

I went to my room to paint my toenails.

I was on nail number four when the doorbell rang.

I padded out to the door and opened it.

Mortimer was standing there, looking scared. That's his regular look. I wish I could help him with that, but he hasn't asked me.

"It's my turn to take Feathers for his walk," he said. "We're going to Alta Plaza Park."

I got Feathers and handed the cage to
Mortimer. "You two enjoy your walk."

I went back to my toenails.

I was giving nail number two a second
coat when the doorbell rang.

Mortimer was back. He tiptoed in and
closed the door.

"A kid with a big hat followed me down in the elevator," he said. "He asked me who the canary belonged to. I didn't tell him."

I laughed. "That's E.J. He thinks he's a spy. He's new in the building."

"He's new at school, too," Mortimer said. "I've seen him talking to Desiree a lot."

"Oh, no!" I said. "We're in big trouble. I bet Desiree *hired* him to find out what her

feathered present from you and Sheena and
Duncan is. And now he's seen you with
Feathers!"

"And he's waiting to see me some more,"
Mortimer said. "He's downstairs, hiding
behind a plant."

Now I knew I had a *real* case! And I
knew what I had to do.

I grabbed Feathers's
cage. "Feathers
is staying in," I said.
"You're taking *Hoot*
to the park. Lead the
spy *away* from this
building. If he asks you
about Hoot,

tell him you've got a bird-walking
service."

I got Hoot, gave her to Mortimer, and
pushed him out the door.

chapter thirteen
Face to Face

There wasn't time to start a file on the case. I rang for Willie.

"Back to the Feathered Friends Pet Shop," I said as I stepped into the limo.

When we got to the pet store I dashed inside, pointing in all directions.

"Do you rent?" I asked. "Never mind, I'll take one of each."

I got back in the limo with a duck, a parrot, and a turkey.

"You're going overboard for birds, Boss," Willie said as the duck tried to waddle around the front seat.

Back home I had Willie check to make sure the elevator was empty.

E.J. was not in sight.

The birds and I made the trip to the top without any problems, except for some squawking and quacking.

Mrs. Fridgeflake eyed them nervously. "More overnight guests?"

I put the birds in the blue room in back. "I'll come for you soon," I promised them, and I closed the door.

Ten minutes later Mortimer rang the bell. "We were followed every step of the way," he whispered. "Is our secret safe or unsafe?"

"Soon it will be safe," I said.

Mortimer handed Hoot to me and left.

I put Hoot in the yellow room with
Feathers. "No fighting," I warned.

I went to my office, grabbed my red
telephone, and dialed 555-4133.

"E.J.'s Spy Service," a voice answered.
"This is E.J."

"This is Olivia Sharp."

"Hi, Liver. I know one of your secrets."

"Do you?"

"Sure. That's
my job.
Mortimer,
Sheena, and
Duncan got a
birthday present

for Desiree and you're keeping it for them."

I tapped my pencil on my desk. "Am I?"

"Listen, Liver. Desiree hinted for a present with feathers. And they got her a canary. Or an owl. Either way it's a pretty weird birthday present, if you ask me."

"I didn't ask. And don't you dare come up here to look around!"

I slammed down the receiver.

I was smiling. I knew it wouldn't be long before my doorbell rang.

It wasn't.

He was there at the big door, big hat
and all.

"Stay out," I said, leaving the door open
wide enough for him to squeeze his way in.
He was now dealing, face to face, with
Olivia Sharp, Agent for Secrets.

chapter fourteen

Feathered Confusion

E.J. started to walk around my penthouse.

Chirping sounds and hoots were coming from the yellow room.

He headed straight for it, walked in, and

saw Feathers and Hoot. "One of these is Desiree's present," he said. "All I have to do is figure out which one."

I slipped away while E.J. went on talking.

I walked down the hall, opened the door to the blue room, and said, "Okay, birds, you're free!"

I was back before E.J. knew I was gone.

He was still staring at Hoot, then Feathers, then back at Hoot again.

A duck waddled past me into the room, quacking happily. Behind it a turkey gobble-gobbled. A parrot flew in, squawking. Feathers chirped. Hoot kept her beak shut. Sometimes she's so stuck-up.

E.J. looked from the duck to the turkey to

the parrot and then back to the canary and
the owl.

I *love* confusion, especially when I
cause it.

E.J. did not know which bird was
the present!

My plan had worked. The secret
was safe.

E.J. pushed his hat back. "Clever work,
Liver, but I still know the present is a *bird*!
So there!"

I had to think fast.

I said, "Let's go to my office."

I think faster there.

I led the way.

chapter fifteen

Spilling the Secret . . . Maybe

"Nice place," E.J. said, fingering my red phone.

We sat down.

E.J. was chuckling. "A bird is a really

weird present," he said. "Especially if it's a turkey. Weird presents are the greatest. I wanted to get Desiree something weird but I couldn't find anything."

I looked E.J. straight in the eye. "What *are* you giving Desiree for her birthday?"

He squirmed. Then he said, "That's my secret until she opens it. I want her to be surprised."

"See?" I said. "Even *you* know that birthday secrets should be kept."

I leaned toward him. "Listen to me, E.J. I don't know how long you've been a spy, but there are some cases you shouldn't take. You think *I* take every case that comes along?"

So far I had. But they were all good causes.

I put my feet up on my desk. "We both want Desiree to have a happy birthday, right?"

E.J. was staring or glaring at me. Hard to tell which.

"I worked hard on this case," he said. "You want me to drop it?"

"Your choice." I pointed to my red telephone. "You can use this to call Desiree."

I tapped my fingers on my desk while E.J. dialed. Was he going to spill the bird secret?

It seemed to take forever for Desiree to answer.

Then E.J. spoke into the phone. "E.J.'s Spy Service reporting in," he said. "I finished the case. Got the big answer. You'll

love this, Desiree. Your birthday present
is—"

I didn't want to hear it!

"WEIRD!" he announced. "Glad I could
be of help."

E.J. hung up.

chapter sixteen
Tea for Two

E.J. wasn't so bad after all.

I invited him for tea. He took off his hat
and stayed.

He called me Liver twice, but I let it pass.

After he left, I went to my office and
called Sheena.

"All's well," I said.

For her and Duncan and Mortimer it
was. For me, I had to plan a future for a
duck, a turkey, and a parrot.

I started and finished a file on the case.

This is how I ended it:

* TOMORROW DESIREE IS GETTING A CANARY FROM SHEENA, DUNCAN, AND MORTIMER.

* SHE'S GETTING BANGLES FROM ME AND A PIN WITH HER NAME ON IT FROM E.J.
** HE DOESN'T KNOW I SAW THE ORDER FORM STICKING OUT OF HIS POCKET.

E.J. HAS A LOT MORE TO LEARN ABOUT BEING A SPY. AND A FRIEND.

MAYBE I'LL TEACH HIM.

MAYBE I WON'T.

Then I wrote to my cousin.

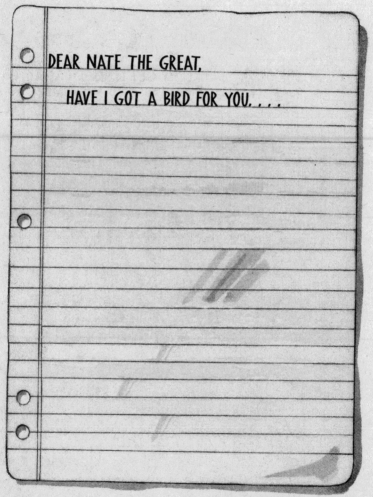

DEAR NATE THE GREAT,

HAVE I GOT A BIRD FOR YOU. . . .